Chapter 1
A Trip to the Library

Amanda and her brother, Brian, love reading. They read many books. They like funny books and silly books. They also like scary books.

"Good morning, Miss Martins!" Amanda and Brian say.

"Good morning, children!" replies Miss Martins, the librarian.

"Which book do you want to read today?" asks Miss Martins.

"We want to read *THE GROWLY MONSTER*," answer the children.

Amanda and Brian sit at a round
table and wait. They are excited.
They wait and wait and wait.
Miss Martins brings them the book,
but there is something wrong.

"What happened to the letters?" shouts Amanda.

"Where are the pictures?" asks Brian.

The pages of the book are empty.
They are silent and white.
The children are sad. The children
are shocked.

Chapter 2

Looking for Letters and Pictures

"Who took the letters?" cries Amanda.

"Who took the pictures?" asks Brian.

Amanda stands on her two small feet. "We must find the letters," she says.

"We must find the pictures," Brian says.

The children think carefully. They search the library, but they don't find anything. They must look in the garden.

Amanda takes binoculars and a big empty bag. Brian has a butterfly net.

"Are you ready, Brian?" asks Amanda.

"Yes, Amanda, let's go!" says Brian.

Amanda walks in front. Brian follows behind her. They look over the bushes. They look under the leaves. They look in the flowers. They look everywhere, but they cannot find the words and the pictures.

Chapter 3
Time to Rest

The day is hot. The children are tired. Amanda looks for a cool place to rest. She chooses a shady tree. Amanda and Brian sit down. They drink water.

Amanda lies down on the cool grass. She looks up through the branches of the tree and into the sky.

"Look, Brian," points Amanda, "the letters are up there!"

Brian looks up and sees frightened letters sitting on top of the highest branches.

"What are you doing there?" asks Brian.

Slowly the letters move around and make words. Then the words make a sentence **"WE ARE HIDING."**

"Why are you hiding?" asks Amanda.

The letters move again, and new words make a new sentence **"WE ARE SCARED."**

"Why are you scared?" asks Brian.

Once again, the letters move around and make another sentence **"WE ARE SCARED OF THE GROWLY MONSTER."**

"What did he do?" Amanda asks.

"**HE TOOK US AWAY FROM OUR HOME IN THE STORYBOOK**," the letters say.

"Oh!" says Amanda. "We can take you home. Jump into my big bag," Amanda says.

The letters float down into the big bag.

"But where are the pictures?" asks Brian.

"We must keep looking," says Amanda.

Chapter 4
Butterflies

The children look everywhere, but they cannot find the pictures.

"Where are the pictures?" asks Amanda.

"Look!" points Brian. "That picture is riding on a butterfly."

Brian swings his butterfly net and catches the picture. It is a picture of flowers. The flowers are scared.

"Why are you scared?" asks Brian.

"The Growly Monster took us away from our home in the storybook," reply the flowers.

"Get into my big bag," says Amanda. "I will take you back to your home."

Another picture is on another
butterfly.

"Look, there's the picture of the
fairy!" shouts Amanda.

"But where is the Growly Monster?" asks Brian.

"The Growly Monster is under the mushroom," whispers the fairy from the book.

Chapter 5
Not Just a Monster

Amanda and Brian look under the giant mushroom.

"What are you doing there?" asks Amanda.

"Why did you take all the letters and pictures away from their home in the storybook?" asks Brian.

"I was angry!" says the Growly Monster.

"Why were you angry?" asks Amanda.

"I was angry because I was made a book monster. No one loves an ugly monster. I wish to be handsome and fluffy!" says the Growly Monster.

"Don't be silly, Growly Monster," says Amanda. "We love you just the way you are, and we want you back in the storybook."

"You love me? Even if I am a monster?" asks the Growly Monster.

"Of course we do! We love you for what you are. And we want you back!" Amanda says.

"Yes! We want the story back," says Brian.

"I am sorry," says the Growly Monster. "I will rescue the story for you."

Amanda and Brian take the Growly Monster and the letters and the words and the sentences and the pictures back to their home inside the pages of the storybook.

The Growly Monster and Fairy . . . . .

The Growly Monster is happy now. He is back in the storybook where he is loved for who he is.

Amanda and Brian read their favorite storybook. The storybook has everything it should have. It has letters and words and sentences and pictures. Most importantly, it has the Growly Monster.